Letting Go

Letting Go

Joyce A. Stengel

Illustrations by Marianne Lee

POOLBEG
FOR CHILDREN

Published 1997 by
Poolbeg Press Ltd
123 Baldoyle Industrial Estate
Dublin 13, Ireland

© Joyce A. Stengel 1997

The moral right of the author has been asserted.

A catalogue record for this book is available from the British Library.

ISBN 1 85371 761 4

Illustrations by Marianne Lee
Cover design by Poolbeg Group Services Ltd
Set by Poolbeg Group Services Ltd in Times 12/18
Printed by The Guernsey Press Ltd,
Vale, Guernsey, Channel Islands.

About the Author

Joyce A. Stengel lives with her husband in Rocky Hill, Connecticut. They have two grown daughters and two grandchildren. She has written numerous articles which have appeared in various American magazines and newspapers. She is the author of *The Caribbean Jewels Mystery* published by Poolbeg.

For my husband, Bob
For Dr Casey

Contents

Chapter One
Another Foster Home

Mrs Cruz's car rattled through the frozen streets to the highway entrance. We passed suburbs, then the city. Traffic whizzed by us. Warm air swooshed from the noisy heater and swirled around my ankles and in my face. I felt like I was in a little cocoon, sort of between two worlds. I wished I could stay there. I didn't want to go to another foster-home. I wanted my mother.

Mrs Cruz lectured me. "Kathy. Listen to me. You must learn to control those tantrums. Mr and Mrs O'Neil are what – the sixth or seventh foster-parents in only four years that couldn't put up with your temper. That's always the reason I have to find a new place for you. You're ten years old, old enough to control yourself. There's no excuse for such outbursts."

No excuse? What about Michelle taunting, "You're only a foster-child – a reject. You don't have a real mother – reject, reject," all the way home on the school bus? I'd tried. I'd really tried to control myself. But I couldn't. Every so often, rage just seemed to fly out of me, like a volcano erupting. It frightened me.

Oh, how I wished I were going back to my own mother. Then I'd be me, Kathy James, not "a foster-child." Someday I would go back. Some day soon, I thought, fingering the list of names in my pocket – the list I'd sent for after I saw my mother on MTV. I was sure it was her – long, golden-brown hair, just like mine. I couldn't see her eyes. I wondered if they were brown with little yellow specks, like mine. I couldn't remember.

Mrs Cruz's voice droned on, but I tuned her out. I was thinking of another winter four years ago when I was six. It was after Christmas then, too.

Mommy, her legs crossed and one foot swinging back and forth so fast it made a breeze, was shouting into the telephone. "I've got the kid. How can I go? . . . Oh, Charlie, it sounds wonderful. Do you really think I'd get it? . . . Well, I don't know. No, no, there's no one I can leave her with, but . . ."

I remember her squinting at me through cigarette smoke, then stabbing the cigarette out like she hated it. "Yeah, I know. I know I said I'd do it, but . . . It does sound like a great chance. Maybe you're right," she said, standing up and looking away from me. "If I don't do it now, when will I? Listen, I'll talk to you later, Charlie."

I watched her hang up the phone and stare at it, my stomach warning me something bad was about to happen. She dashed into her room and pulled a suitcase out from under the bed. "Come on, Kathy, you're packing."

"Where are we going, Mommy?" I asked, clutching Bozo, the brown, fuzzy teddy bear she'd given me for Christmas.

"I'm going with Charlie. He's got a spot for me at a high-class place in Vegas. They need a singer."

"I don't like Charlie."

"You're going to live with someone else."

"No," I cried, stamping my foot. "No! No!"

"Yes. Yes. I've put my life on hold long enough. Now it's my turn."

Before I knew it, we were getting off the bus in the city, my mother carrying the suitcase, me carrying Bozo. I followed her through the icy streets, wondering where we were going. She hurried up the steps of a brick building. "Come on, Kathy, move it! I'm freezing," she yelled back at me.

Inside, I dragged behind my mother down a hallway to a door with a glass window. She opened the door and we were in a room where a lady with white hair sat behind a desk. My mother talked to her in a fast, low voice. The lady opened another door and we were in a tiny room without windows. That was the first time I saw Mrs Cruz.

Mrs Cruz bumped down an exit that read "Middleboro". She turned left at the end of the ramp and drove under the highway. The narrow road twisted this way and that and then we were in the country. There were gigantic snowdrifts and black skeleton woods. We passed a post office not far back from the road. Then more woods. A church. More woods.

"Kathy? You're not listening to me," Mrs Cruz complained.

"Yes, I am," I said. She'd been talking on and on about Pat Hartwell. How her husband had died two years ago, how she owned a coffee shop with someone called Jeremiah Tyler, how she had a son . . .

A son! The words knotted my stomach and prickles of anger shot through me. I thought of the son, Tom, in the foster-home before the last – how he was always snitching money from his parents and how they always blamed me. I was the foster-kid. Their very own son

4

couldn't be a thief. Well, I'd keep my distance from this son. I'd be gone by spring, anyway. I just had to write that letter and my mother would come for me.

"Please behave yourself this time, Kathy. Pat Hartwell is taking you as a big favour to me. She's been very busy with her restaurant, but she . . ."

I clenched my fists and swung my head towards her. "It's not like I *want* to go live with her. I want to live with my mother, but nobody will listen to me."

Mrs Cruz heaved a great exasperated sigh. "Kathy, we haven't heard a thing from your mother in four years."

"She'll come back for me," I insisted. "She promised."

Mrs Cruz frowned and her hands tightened on the steering wheel. "Just don't give Pat Hartwell a hard time."

The car crested a hill and started down. Trees arched from steep, snow-covered banks, blocking the pale winter sun.

Suddenly, Mrs Cruz started pumping the brakes. "Oh, dear! We're skidding."

Down, down we tunnelled. Then WHUMP!

Heavy white snow blocked my window and lay in great clumps on the hood of the car, making me feel as though I were in a strange land. I wasn't a bit hurt, but I felt kind of dazed. I watched Mrs Cruz push her great mass of hair from her face. She turned and stared at me, her large, dark eyes popping like a frog's. "Well, here we are. That's the house, right across the street."

She jockeyed the car back and forth until she freed it, then steered into the driveway on the left side of the street. The car chugged up the curving drive to an old, stone house with green trim and spluttered to a stop.

I fiddled with my seat belt, wishing I didn't have to leave the warm car, wishing I were a normal kid, not a foster-child.

"Come on, Kathy. It's cold out here," Mrs Cruz called, her breath making little grey puffs.

I stepped out into the cold, then got my suitcase out of the back seat and, shivering, looked around. A shovelled path led to the back door. A lopsided snowman stood in the yard that stopped at a low stone wall. Snowy steps led up to the yard in the back, where naked trees stretched out their limbs and shuddered in the wind. A huge, gnarled tree, closest to the wall, stood apart from the others.

"Those are apple trees," Mrs Cruz said. "Just wait till spring when those trees are in blossom. They're beautiful."

6

They're sure ugly now, I thought, and they look lonely, like me, especially that big one. But what did it matter what the apple trees looked like? By spring, I'd be with my mother.

I followed Mrs Cruz up the path, past the lopsided snowman, to the back door. Strangers all over again. My stomach jumped. I felt like a small ball tossed about by big people.

"Come in. Come in," boomed the big woman with smiling grey eyes, who opened the door.

Mrs Cruz gave me a little push into a warm room filled with an apple cinnamon smell that made my mouth water. The room looked like it used to be a porch. The back and side walls were practically all window. Looking out, I could see the bare trees against the white snow. A fluffy, orange cat slept by a wood-burning stove, diagonal to the two window-walls. A worn red and blue plaid couch occupied the far wall, with a table heaped with magazines and books in front of it. To the left of the couch was a table with a lamp and a large picture; a picture of Mrs Hartwell, a man, and a little boy. That must be the son. And the bright-coloured Lego structures spreading from the far side of the couch on to the braided rug must be his. But where was the TV?

"Take off your coat, Kathy," Mrs Hartwell said. "You too, Anita. How about a muffin or a piece of apple pie right from the oven? I made extra today."

Mrs Cruz said she had an appointment and couldn't stay. While the two women talked in low voices, I studied Mrs Hartwell, checking her out. She smiled a lot, especially her eyes. A stretchy red hair-band swept her pale brown hair back from her round face. Would she think of me as "a poor little kid" like Mr and Mrs O'Neil had, or a "troublesome delinquent?" I was pretty good at figuring people out by now, but I couldn't classify her yet. The big smile must be fake. She didn't really want me here. She was just taking me as a favour to Mrs Cruz.

Mrs Cruz picked up her handbag and gloves, then came over to say good-bye. "Give Mrs Hartwell a chance, Kathy. And remember what I said."

"Well, how about that pie now?" Mrs Hartwell asked, shutting the door behind Mrs Cruz. She hurried into the big kitchen to the left of the porch room, where pies and muffins were cooling on the counter. The sweet pastry smell made my stomach growl. But I said, "I'm not hungry. I don't want anything."

"Not hungry? Well, sure you are. I've never seen a kid who couldn't eat a piece of pie and drink a cup of hot chocolate," she said, her long, strong-looking hands setting out plates and mugs.

"I don't want anything," I said. "Can I go to my room?"

"Sure, if that's what you want. I've got to make more muffins or I'd take you up. Jeremiah will be picking up all these baked goods tonight for the Coffee Stop. So you just take your suitcase right on up. The stairs are off the dining-room and your room is right at the top of the stairs."

The back door groaned open, letting in a blast of wind, and a skinny little kid, who looked to be about six, blew in with it. He stopped short when he saw me and stood there, staring at me through steamy owl-like glasses, water pooling beneath his boots. I stared right back at him.

"Hi, Laurence," said Mrs Hartwell, unzipping his jacket and engulfing him in a big hug. He put his bony arms around her neck and hugged her back. A hunger surged through me, different from food hunger.

"Say hello to Kathy James," Mrs Hartwell said. "She just got here."

"Who cares?" he muttered, pulling away from her. By now the room was freezing cold.

"I'm only here because I have to be," I said, squinting my eyes at the horrible little boy. I picked up my suitcase and marched out of the room. This place was going to be the worst yet. I just knew it.

Chapter Two
The Plan

The next morning Mrs H – that's what I decided to call her, not Pat or Aunt Pat like she suggested – drove Laurence and me to school. Her Volkswagen Golf chugged through glittering streets. A night snowfall had frosted everything white. I wished we'd had a blizzard. Then I wouldn't have to face another new school.

When we got to the school, Mrs H heaved herself out of the tiny car. "Watch your step, Kathy; it's real slippery," she said, holding on to Laurence's hand and reaching for mine. I snatched it away. I wasn't a baby, and I wasn't about to walk into a new school holding some lady's hand. Not that I cared what the other kids thought. I wouldn't be here long.

Inside, Laurence reached up his skinny arms and Mrs H bent down and hugged him, then he walked down a hallway, his lunch box banging against his leg.

"Now, we'll get you settled in, Kathy, then I'm off to the Coffee Stop. Tonight you'll meet Jeremiah, my friend and partner," she said, smiling down at me.

I nodded but didn't say anything as we walked to the principal's office.

"Mrs Cruz tells me you're a whiz in maths. Maybe you can help Laurence with his numbers."

No way, I thought. He didn't like me and I didn't like him, and that was that.

When Mrs H left me with Ms Ficara, the principal, my stomach knotted. Ms Ficara was tall and thin and seemed to be in a hurry. As she walked me to my classroom, I kept thinking how to ask something really important to me. She talked fast, explaining that Mrs Levine would look over the report from my other school and give me some tests. For now, I was to pay attention and try to pick up where the other students were. I'd heard it all before.

She stopped outside a door and raised her knuckles to knock. My heart thumping, I cleared my throat and blurted, "Ms Ficara, please don't tell I'm a foster-child."

Her hand still poised to knock, she looked down at

me. She studied me a moment, then said, "I have to tell Mrs Levine, but I'll ask her not to tell the other children." Her knuckles rapped the door.

Mrs Levine opened the door and, raising her eyebrows high, stared at us. I stood still as a statue while they talked in a murmur. Why did adults do that – whisper about me as though I wasn't even there? Mrs Levine swept her glasses from the top of her head where they nestled in grey curls and clicked the bows back and forth. I heard her mutter, " . . . twenty-five! Such a big class." Ms Ficara shrugged a "What can I do?" shrug and nodded toward me. "Kathy's a foster-child, but she'd like that information to remain between the three of us."

Mrs Levine slid her glasses on and, pursing her lips and frowning, studied me. Suddenly she smiled and her stern face brightened. "OK. It's our secret."

She drew me into the room and introduced me to the class. "You can sit right over there, behind Megan Flanagan," she said, pointing to a desk behind a girl with a mop of red hair.

I felt everyone staring at me. Here I was, the new kid, starting at a new school in the middle of January. I lifted my head and gazed straight ahead.

We had maths, and I was soon lost in the world of

numbers, nice logical numbers. Then Mrs Levine said we should write an essay about someone we knew. "Choose a family member, your mother or father, or maybe a sister or brother or an aunt or uncle. Try to make that person seem real, so real that when someone reads your essay they'll feel they know that person."

She snapped open a gold watch that hung from a chain around her neck. "You have time to get started before lunch. Finish them tonight. They're due tomorrow morning." She clicked the gold watch shut and sat down to a stack of papers on her desk.

I looked around the room. Most of the kids had already started to write. Megan was hunched over her paper, scribbling like lightning.

"Good cook," said a boy in the front of the room.

"Write it down, Jason," said Mrs Levine. "No talking."

I stared out the window and chewed on my pencil. Who could I write about?

I drew some shapes – squares, diamonds, circles, then stick people. Who could I write about? I looked at the stick people, a mother and little girl holding hands. *Mommy, Mommy, Mommy* beat in my head like a drum. I wrote – *beautiful, sings and dances.* I looked at the words. What else could I say? *Has to travel a lot. Writes to me. Sends me great presents. Misses me . . . misses me.*

14

The bell rang. Chairs scraped and everyone surged toward the door. In the lunchroom, I got milk to drink with my lunch and hurried over to an empty table, not looking at anyone.

"Hi, new girl," said the boy named Jason, plunking his tray down opposite mine.

"Hi," I answered. He was funny-looking. Big teeth and one of those skinny little ponytails that grew from the back of his head. He shovelled macaroni and cheese into his mouth.

Megan and another girl came over and sat opposite each other, Megan next to me.

"Your name's Kathy, right?" Megan said.

I nodded.

"I'm Megan and this is Kim," she said.

Kim looked like a china doll with blue eyes and long black hair. She stared at me, her blue eyes hardly blinking. "Hi," she said, pulling out a chair. Her perfect smile showed a glimpse of even white teeth.

"That's Pigpen," Megan continued, rolling her green eyes and pointing at Jason.

Jason opened his mouth wide and stuck out his cheese-coated tongue.

"Yuck! You're gross!" Megan unwrapped a ham and cheese sandwich. "Wow! You've got lots of goodies,"

15

she said to me. She smacked her lips and bit into her sandwich. Mrs H had packed a tuna sandwich, carrot and celery sticks, and a huge supply of brownies.

"Boys are always gross," Kim said, giving Jason a scornful look. China Doll and Raggedy Ann, I thought, looking from Kim to Megan with her mane of red hair.

"Can I have one?" asked Jason, reaching for a brownie.

"Sure," I said, pushing the plastic bag towards him. "There's enough here for everyone."

"I'll try one," said Megan. "Your mother sure packs a yummy lunch."

"My mother didn't pack this. Mrs H, the lady I'm staying with, did."

"Mrs H? How come you call her that?" Kim asked, closing her lips on a spoonful of yogurt.

"Just a nickname."

Jason, his mouth full, mumbled, "Where's your mother? Did she die?"

"No, my mother's a movie star. She sings and dances. I saw her on television. She travels all around. She wanted me to go with her because she misses me so much, but . . . school, you know. She comes for me whenever she can. I'm just staying with Mrs H till my mother gets back," I said, the words rolling out of my mouth.

I wasn't really lying. After all, I'd seen my mother on MTV. And I was sure she would have me with her if she could. Anyway, I didn't want them to know I was a foster-child. I just wanted to be a regular kid — not a reject.

Megan drained the last of her chocolate milk and wiped her mouth. "Cool! Just think . . . a movie star for a mother!"

"I suppose you're going to write about her. What television programme is she on?" Kim asked, neatly peeling a banana."

"MTV."

"Oh. My mother won't let me watch that," Kim said, arching her fine eyebrows.

Megan shot Kim a look, then said, "Kathy, do you sing, too? You could try out for the spring play. I hear it's going to be *Alice in Wonderland*."

Kim tossed her gleaming black hair over her shoulder. "I'm trying out for Alice. I had the lead in last year's play. The programme will say: 'Kim Sipes as Alice'."

"Maybe I'll try out for the White Rabbit," Jason said, biting into another brownie. Suddenly, he stroked his little pigtail. "The programme will say: 'Jason Martinez as the White Rabbit'."

"You've got the teeth for it," Kim snapped, glaring at him.

Megan snickered.

I kept thinking about what Megan had said. I had sung solos before. It was strange. I hated to talk in class, but it was different on stage. When I was on stage, I wasn't me. I was somebody else.

What if I were in the play? What if I were Alice? Maybe . . . my mother would come. I could see her in the audience, smiling up at me.

I thought of the list of names hidden under the pink-and-white striped paper in my bottom drawer. Monica James wasn't on it, but Monica Starr was. That must be my mother's movie star name. I just knew it. If I were Alice . . . why, then . . . my mother would really want to see me. If I were Alice . . . my mother would come back for me.

Chapter Three
Putting the Plan in Action

The bus creaked to a stop and Laurence and I jumped down the steps into an icy wind. I clutched my books close and hurried up the driveway, Laurence trudging behind me.

Laurence's cry made me turn around. He raced to his snowman, whose head lay in a heap on the ground, shrieking, "My snowman! My snowman! Who smashed my snowman?"

I kicked at a pile of slush. "Nerd! It got warmer today and his head slid off."

He pushed at his glasses with his mittened hands and scowled at me. "I bet you knocked his head off."

"Yeah. Sure. Right." I left Laurence repairing Mr Snowman and hurried into the house. Marmalade, the fluffy orange cat, looked up from her spot near the wood-burning stove and meowed a complaint about the

cold air. Then she tucked her head under her paws and went back to sleep.

"How was the first day of school?" Mrs H called from the kitchen.

"OK," I mumbled.

"Want some milk and blueberry muffins?"

"I don't want anything," I said, ignoring my rumbling stomach.

"Well, go ahead and change. Then you can don an apron and peel some apples for me. Four apple pies and I'll be done for the day. Jeremiah will be over later to pick these goodies up for the Coffee Stop. He's looking forward to meeting you."

"I have homework to do." I really wanted to watch TV. I watched a lot at the O'Neil's, hoping to see my mother again. But there wasn't even one TV in this house.

Mrs H shot me a look through the kitchen door. Her round face looked flushed and warm. "Don't want to peel apples, huh? OK for today, but I expect you to help with the chores around here."

From my back window, the woods looked blue-cold and dreary. Laurence was still out there, trying to make another snowman. His wrists and bare hands looked like sticks poking out of the ends of his puffy snowsuit.

I shivered. The bedrooms were cold in this old house. I draped my worn flannel bathrobe across my shoulders and sat cross-legged on the bed, Bozo on my lap. I stared at the paper in front of me. My mother . . . how should I start? At least my mother wouldn't treat me like a slave and make me peel apples, like Mrs H. I chewed the eraser on my pencil for a while then wrote, "My mother . . ." Memories flooded through me.

"You're not able to take care of your daughter, any more?" Mrs Cruz said to my mother. "Why don't you have her wait in the other office, and we'll talk about it."

"No," my mother said, pressing her mouth into a tight, thin line, twisting her hands round each other. "There's nothing more to say. She's old enough to understand. I just can't take care of myself and a kid, too. It's impossible."

"*What about her father?*" Mrs Cruz looked at me. I squirmed and held Bozo tight.

"*Her father took off before she was born. The last I heard he was dead, and that's fine with me. The only thing he ever did for me was to leave me in a mess. There's her suitcase. It's got all her clothes in it.*" She knelt down to give me a hug. "*Bye, Kathy. Be good. No temper tantrums or nobody will want you.*"

I stood still in her arms. "Mommy, let's go home now."

She stood up and shook back her golden hair. "Kathy, you're going to live with other people. It will be better for you."

"*I want to live with you.*" *My voice sounded funny from the tears in my throat.*

"*I just can't make it with a kid,*" *she said, looking at Mrs Cruz.*

"*I can take care of myself. I won't be in the way.*"

"*Look, I've got to do this, Kathy. I'll come back. OK?*"

She picked up her black handbag and left, her heels clicking on the bare floor.

The sound of the hall floor creaking woke me up. A knock sounded on the door. I rubbed my face . . .

where was I? Mrs H opened the door a crack and peeked in. "Supper's just about ready. Brrrr. It's cold up here."

I was freezing, and I felt all hollow inside. I grabbed Bozo and followed Mrs H down the narrow staircase that led to the dining-room. It was a crazy old house, but kind of neat. The dining-room led into what Mrs H called the first parlour and, to the right of that, was a smaller room, the second parlour. She said it was nice and cool in the summer, but right now it was like a

refrigerator. A door in the first parlour opened on to a small balcony at the front of the house. From there, you could see way out, past the road and over the trees, to the city in the distance.

Laurence, on hands and knees in the porch room, worked on his spreading Lego village near the couch. He looked up, glared at me through his owl glasses,

then went back to building. I don't know why he hated me. But what did I care? I wouldn't be here long. I made a face at his back, set Bozo on the back window-sill and headed for Marmalade, curled up in her usual spot. Her fur felt like a warm coat, and her purrs vibrated right through my hand.

At supper, Laurence didn't say much, just picked at his meat loaf and mashed potatoes. He looked so miserable, I almost felt sorry for him. Mrs H talked about how busy it was at the Coffee Stop at lunch, then started questioning me – the usual stuff, did I like Mrs Levine? How were the other kids? If I wanted to invite somebody over after school, I could.

I took a deep breath. Now was the time to put my plan into action. If I got a part in the play, I had to be sure I could stay for rehearsals.

"There's going to be a spring play. Maybe I'll try out," I said in a rush. I held my breath, waiting for her answer.

Mrs H looked up from her plate. "Why, that's great," she said.

"There'd be lots of rehearsals," I said. "I'd have to stay after school. I wouldn't be able to peel apples every day."

Mrs H smiled. "We'd work it out."

I waved my fork in the air. "My mother's a singer, you know. I look like her and maybe I sing like her, too."

Laurence pushed his glasses up on his sharp little nose. "If you've got your own mother, how come you're here?"

Mrs H put her fork down and, looking at Laurence, said sternly, "She's here because this is her home now, just like it's yours."

Laurence jumped up, knocking over his chair. "This isn't her home. It's my home."

"Laurence!"

"Why did she have to come? I hate her," he screamed, and ran, crying, from the kitchen.

Just as Mrs H pushed her chair back, a loud hammering shook the door. "Now what?" she mumbled, hurrying to the door and pulling it open. A large, bulky man with white hair and bushy white eyebrows flew in in a flurry of snow.

Mrs H stepped back. "Jeremiah. What's the matter?"

Jeremiah Tyler strode into the room wringing his big, red hands. His black boots spattered great chunks of gritty ice and snow and made Laurence's Lego jump on the floor. "Maisie's gone! I can't find her anywhere!"

Chapter Four
Out of Here by Spring

Mr Tyler clasped his chapped hands together and paced back and forth. "I heard the most horrible yowling. I rushed out but no sign of Maisie. I bet that big tom got her."

Mrs H shut the door. "Now, Jeremiah, calm down! Your blood pressure. I'm sure Maisie's all right. She probably just chased that old tomcat off your property – you know, her territory."

"I've searched all around my place. No sign of her. She may be hurt. I'm going to look around your yard. She likes those apple trees. Got a torch I can use?"

Rustling through a kitchen drawer, Mrs H pulled out a torch. "I'll help you. Kathy, check on Laurence. See if he's all right."

Mrs H struggled into her parka, pulled on her boots, then the two of them hurried out the door into the cold.

I sat there, stunned. Check on Laurence! I was the last person he'd want to see. He wanted her, not me. Adults! Who could understand them?

I piled the dishes in the dishwasher and scrubbed the pots and pans. When I finished, they still weren't back. The house was so quiet, I could hear Marmalade purring from her snug place by the stove. I opened the door and peered out into the black night. Shivering, I listened to the wind rattling through the trees. It was no night for a cat to be out. I hoped they'd find her soon.

I closed the door and leaned against it. "Why should I check on Laurence?" I asked aloud. Marmalade opened her eyes a bit, then closed them. Bozo's glass eyes stared back at me from where he sat on the windowsill. Maybe Laurence has a teddy bear like me, I thought. Then he wouldn't need anybody.

A great breath rushed from me as I climbed the stairs. I stepped over the squeaky fourth one, and stood in the hall. There were three bedrooms, Mrs H's in the front and Laurence's to the left of mine in the back. Standing outside his door, I could hear muffled sobs. I knocked. The room got quiet.

Turning the knob and opening the door a crack, I said, "Can I come in?" "No," said Laurence in a choked voice.

I pushed the door wide and, in a shaft of light from the hall, saw him sitting on the edge of his bed, rubbing his sleeve across his nose. He looked so young. About the age I was when my mother left, I thought. I swallowed against the tightness in my throat.

I leaned against the door jamb. "Hey, Laurence, did you get your snowman fixed?" I said.

"Where's my mother?" he mumbled, not looking up.

"She's helping Mr Tyler find his cat."

He didn't say a word, just sat there plucking a loose thread on the bedspread. His room was tidy, books and toy cars neatly arranged in a bookcase under the window. On top of the bookcase sat a duplicate of the picture downstairs: Laurence, Mrs H and a man – his father, I guessed. I wondered what it would be like to have a father. My mother had never talked about mine.

I cleared my throat, afraid my voice would squeak, and said, "I guess you don't want me around."

He squinted at me. Without glasses, his eyes looked tired and weak. "I'm not the only one," he mumbled.

"What do you mean?" I asked.

Laurence's sharp little chin jutted out. "Uncle Jerry doesn't want you here, either. You're ruining everything. Uncle Jerry and Mommy would get married if you weren't here. Then we'd be a real family."

I ran my thumb over my fingernails, feeling their ragged ends. "Yeah. Well, don't worry about me being here long. I plan to be out of here real quick."

"You do?" he asked, picking up his glasses from the bed and fitting them in place. "When are you leaving?"

I stared at him. "I've got a plan."

"What is it?"

"Promise not to tell your mother?"

He nodded, his face still and serious.

"Well . . ." I took a deep breath and grasping the door moulding in either hand, leaned into the room. "I'm going to try out for the school play. Then my mother will come to see me. And I'll leave with her." There. I'd said it. Now it was real.

Laurence squinted up his eyes and fixed them on me. "What if you don't get a part?"

I hugged my hands against the sudden knot in my stomach. "I will."

"But what if you don't?"

My voice rose. "I said I will. I have to. I'll leave in a few months. I promise."

Never moving his eyes from my face, Laurence said, "Cross your heart and hope to die?"

I crossed my heart. "Cross my heart and hope to die."

Downstairs, the door creaked open and we heard Mrs H and Mr Tyler stomping snow from their boots.

"They're back," Laurence shouted, jumping off the bed and flying past me.

I followed slowly and stopped just outside the porch room door. Laurence flung himself into Mrs H's arms, and clung to her. Her face lit with joy, and I got that familiar achy feeling watching them.

"My, my," Mrs H laughed, "what a great hug. Looks like you're feeling better. Did you and Kathy get everything straightened out?"

Mr Tyler put down Maisie, a small grey-and-white cat, and, breathing heavily, pulled off his boots. Free, Maisie glided over to Marmalade and sniffed at her. Marmalade arched her back and hissed.

"Hey," shouted Laurence. "Looks like Marmalade doesn't want Maisie here."

"Marmalade doesn't want her territory invaded," Mr Tyler said, picking up Maisie and cradling her on the ledge of his stomach.

Spotting me, Mrs H smiled and said, "Kathy, come in here and meet Jeremiah and Maisie."

Mrs H detoured to the kitchen. "Jeremiah, say hello to Kathy. She's come to stay with us for a bit. I'll put water on for a good hot cup of tea."

Mr Tyler's tired-looking brown eyes met mine. "Hi there, Kathy. Guess I stirred up a bit of excitement tonight. Maisie here had me all upset."

"Hi," I mumbled. "I . . . I better go upstairs and finish my homework."

"Homework? Got to have a little snack first. Feed the inner man, then you can think better, I always say. Why don't you give Pat a hand with the food? I think I'll sit down and catch my breath." He settled his weight on the plaid couch with a weary sigh.

All they want me to do is work around here, I thought, carrying in a plate of cookies and Danish pastries, then traipsing back for two mugs of hot chocolate, one for Laurence, who sat right by the warm stove, cooing over Marmalade. I looked around for Maisie and spotted a sprig of whiskers and a heart-shaped nose peeking out from behind the blue chair by the door. I took a cookie and my hot chocolate and sat on the edge of the blue chair.

Mrs H set two mugs of steaming tea on the table, sat down beside Mr Tyler, then hunched forward and spooned sugar into one of the mugs. "Two sugars, Jeremiah, or have you cut down to one?"

"One. That'll do. Thank you, dear," he said taking the mug and wrapping his big red hands around it. "What's that you're building tonight, Laurence?" he asked, pointing the mug at the Lego.

"A castle, Uncle Jerry," Laurence said, crawling to the table and choosing a cookie. "Want to help me?"

I stood up and, feeling invisible, mumbled, "I really have to finish my homework. It's due tomorrow."

"Take your chocolate with you, Kathy. It will keep you warm in that draughty room," Mrs H said.

"Night, Kathy," Mr Tyler mumbled around a mouthful of pastry that crumbled on to his chest. "Careful you don't spill that. Pat has enough cleaning to do."

Choking back my anger, I stamped into the kitchen and poured the hot drink down the sink. As I left the kitchen, I heard Laurence's thin voice, "Come on, Uncle Jerry, build with me."

Spring. Spring. The word chanted in my head as I climbed the stairs. I'd be out of here by spring.

Chapter Five
The Dream

February rain pelted the windows, but it was snug and warm in the kitchen. Delicious, hot air rushed from the oven when I opened the door to remove a tin of cranberry muffins.

"Sure smells good, Kathy," said Mrs H, who sat at the kitchen table looking through magazines and cookbooks. "I think your muffins are lighter than mine. Soon, I'll have to get you one of those chef hats."

I placed the tin on a wire rack for the muffins to cool. I'd been here a month already, and I actually liked baking, but I didn't tell Mrs H. How did I know she wouldn't have me in the kitchen all the time?

So far, Mrs H was OK. She didn't keep at me like some foster-parents, or just ignore me like others. It was kind of comfortable here. My stomach didn't ache so much, and I hadn't had any tantrums.

"Do you like dried apricots, Kathy?" asked Mrs H, studying a recipe. "They're real good for you. Did you know they're called the ambrosia of the gods?"

"They look like shrivelled ears," I said, squirting lemon-scented detergent into the sink.

"Ears! Yuk! I don't want any," piped Laurence from the porch room where he worked with his Lego.

"Shrivelled ears," said Mrs H, dissolving into laughter, "Where do you come up with such notions?"

I grinned and swished my hands through the hot sudsy water. There was lots to do in this house, and Mrs H expected Laurence and me to help. She'd told me about her husband, how he'd been a chef for years, then decided to open the Coffee Stop with Mr Tyler. Things were going pretty well until Mr H died of a heart attack a few years ago. Since then, Mrs H had to do all the baking. She said Laurence had had a hard time accepting his father's death.

My father was dead, too. That's what my mother said. I wondered what he had looked like. At least Laurence had a picture of his father. My mother never showed me a picture of mine. She wouldn't even talk about him. Mrs H opened a drawer and lifted out two dishtowels. "Come on, Laurence, give us a hand with these dishes."

Laurence grumbled, but came into the room and started drying dishes. We weren't friends, but we got along. We sort of circled each other, keeping our own territory.

I started singing, low, under my breath, " . . . in my world" from *Alice*. It was one of my favourite songs. When it wasn't freezing out, I'd practise under the big apple tree near the stone wall. I'd imagine, just like Alice, how things would be in my very own world. The wind would carry my voice through the trees and into the meadow, making the yard my own mysterious wonderland.

"I like that tune," Mrs H said, putting dishes away. "When are try-outs?"

"Next week," I said, a nervous flutter in my stomach. I just had to get the role of Alice. Then I would write to my mother. Then . . .

"Do you think Kathy will get Alice?" Laurence asked, drying a cake pan.

"If I had any say, she would," said Mrs H. "Just look at that face and those big brown eyes." She reached to tweak my chin, but I ducked back. "Talk about expressive. Yes, if I were doing the casting, Kathy would be Alice."

I felt my face flame. Mrs Cruz had once told me I

should learn to hide my feelings better, that my face was an open book that anyone could read. Sometimes, that wasn't so great.

Laurence, his narrow face wrinkled into a frown, pulled on my arm. "What about the music teacher? Do you think he'll let you be Alice, Kathy?" I pulled my arm away.

"How about helping Laurence with his numbers tonight, Kathy?" Mrs H said. "I have to go over to Jeremiah's for a while."

Laurence, his glasses slipping down his nose, shot me a happy grin.

My stomach knotted. Whenever Jeremiah Tyler visited, he bossed me around. Do this. Do that. Be sure to help Pat. Like I was a maid. And lately, Mrs H was spending more and more time at his house. Afterwards, she'd seem kind of quiet, like she was thinking about something. It made me wonder if I'd come home from school one day and find Mrs Cruz there, waiting to take me some place else. That couldn't happen! Not now! I had my plan. Try-outs next week. The role of Alice. And then my mother would come.

"Kathy, what do you say? Could you help Laurence with his numbers?" Mrs H repeated.

I figured she thought Laurence and I were becoming

pals. That that was why he cared if I got the part. I knew different, but I said, "OK, I'll work with him."

That night, after Mrs H had left, I used the Lego to help Laurence with his maths, adding them together, taking them away. It was sort of like counting on your fingers, but it worked. I was tossing the Lego into a canister when Laurence, looking down at the floor, mumbled, "Uh, Kathy, do you want to help me build?"

Laurence had never asked me to build with him before, just Jeremiah Tyler, who, huffing and puffing, would get down on the floor and build with him. I was tempted to say "No," I didn't want to play with kid toys. Anyway, why should I? But I looked at skinny little Laurence waiting for my answer and I just couldn't say no.

The Dream

"What are you making?" I asked, sticking two bright yellow pieces together. Laurence's ideas tumbled out – a kingdom, with a castle, a village, and farms surrounding it. He introduced me to the plastic king and queen and all the villagers. He was really into it. He sure had an imagination, probably from all the stories Mrs H read to him.

On the nights she read to him, he'd snuggle against her on the couch, never once interrupting. Sometimes, I'd flop on the floor next to Marmalade and listen. Mrs H would pat the couch and tell me to sit next to her, but I stayed with Marmalade, stroking her warm fur.

I wondered if my mother used to put her arm around me and read to me. I couldn't remember. I did remember making myself peanut butter sandwiches and sitting in front of the television, its pictures and sounds keeping me company.

Laurence tossed a sheet of Lego illustrations in front of me. "You can use this if you want. I make my own designs now." I looked at the instructions and decided on a small house.

For a time, the click, click of Lego snapping together filled the room. Then Laurence darted to Marmalade, roasting by the wood stove as usual, and pulled her into his lap. "I heard Mommy and Uncle

Jerry talking about Florida the other day. I bet that's where they want to go on their honeymoon. Do you think they'll take me?"

I snorted. "No way. People don't take kids on their honeymoon." I narrowed my eyes and looked at him. "I guess you think I'll get Alice."

His face got serious. "Mommy thinks you will. Anyway, you promised you'd leave by June."

"That's right," I said, pulling my house apart and tossing the pieces into the canister, where they landed with a clank, startling Marmalade and making her dash out of Laurence's arms. "I'll leave by June."

"Yes," Laurence said, nodding his head in satisfaction. "Then Mommy and Uncle Jerry can get married."

That night I dreamt about my mother. She was just ahead of me, her long golden-brown hair floating behind her. I kept running to catch up with her, but I seemed to run in place, going nowhere.

Chapter Six
An Enemy

"I can't wait till music. We finally find out who gets what part," Megan said as she and I slid into chairs opposite Jason in the cafeteria.

"I've been practising wiggling my ears," said Jason, giving us a demonstration.

I opened my lunch bag and took a tiny bite of my sandwich, then put it down. My stomach was such a jumble, I knew I couldn't eat.

Kim, who hadn't been eating with us lately, pulled out the chair next to Jason. She'd been acting smug since the try-outs last week, telling everyone that she would be Alice. And she had been good! Better than I'd ever imagined. Now she lifted her glistening black hair over her shoulders and let it fall down her back. We'd all stopped talking when she sat down, and she spoke into a pool of silence. "My mother's going to call my grandparents tonight to ask them to come see me as Alice."

"Don't be so sure you'll get the part," Megan snapped, chomping a big bite out of her sandwich.

Kim peeled the lid off her yogurt. "It won't be you. That's for sure."

"I bet Kathy gets the part," said Jason, a piece of lettuce stuck on one of his oversized teeth. "And you'll be the Queen of Hearts – the mean queen."

Kim gave him a disgusted look. Then, concentrating on scooping out a spoonful of yogurt, she said, "At least I know my grandparents will come down from Maine just to see me. You know, Kathy, I've been watching for your mother on television, but I've never seen her."

Megan's red hair bristled. "I thought you couldn't watch MTV."

Kim, fixing her blue eyes on me and raising her thin eyebrows, said, "I've been watching it with my mother. We've been looking for Monica Starr. But we haven't seen her."

The knot in my stomach pulled tighter. I squashed my sandwich and stuffed it in the paper bag. "You'll see her the night of the play," I said, hoping I sounded more sure than I felt. I just had to get the part of Alice.

I could just picture it. My mother, all dressed up and beautiful, coming into the auditorium. She'd be the most beautiful mother there. And everyone would know she was *my* mother. Then what would Kim have to say? Oh, if only she hadn't been so good at try-outs.

That afternoon, Mrs Levine clicked open her pendant watch, and looking at it, said, "I know you're all anxious to get to music, but it's journal-writing time." Then, grabbing her watch as it slid down her dress, she cried, "Look at that. The chain broke. Well, I'm glad I caught it. I'd hate for the watch to break." She slid the watch and chain into her cardigan pocket, and said, "OK, get writing."

A stiff March wind rattled the windows and splashed them with rain. Soon, I'd know. I stared at the blank white page of my journal. At first, I'd hated writing in it. But, after Mrs Levine told me she was the only one who'd read it, it was easier. Today, my mind kept turning to the play and Alice.

My blue ballpoint scrawled, "In a way, my life is like Alice's. Every time I go to a new foster-home is like falling down a hole in the ground. I never know who I'll meet or what to expect."

"What's up, doc?" Jason called in a loud whisper, and I knew he couldn't wait for music either.

"Write, Jason," said Mrs Levine. "Save the talk for later."

I looked over at Kim. What was she writing about? How she was sure she'd get the part of Alice. Maybe she would. A lot of the kids thought she would. She'd been so good at try-outs. And she'd had the lead last year. What if she got Alice? Then what? Would my mother come to see me in another role? No. It had to be Alice, the star.

Finally, Mrs Levine pushed her chair back and stood up. "Time for music," she announced. Chairs scraped back and everyone pushed toward the door. "In line. In line," Mrs Levine called. She waited till we quieted down, then we filed out to music class.

We had just reached the auditorium when I realised I'd forgotten my music. I looked around for Mrs Levine. She and Mr Stickles, the music teacher, were talking. Some of the kids called him The Stick, he was so tall and skinny, and a stickler for rules. Every class, he slapped his baton against the palm of his hand, and shouted, "Be prompt. Be prepared. Be attentive." If I asked to run back and get my music in front of him, he would know I wasn't prepared. What should I do? If I had got the part of Alice and he found out I wasn't prepared, would he change his mind? I couldn't ask Mrs Levine in front of him. But I shouldn't leave without permission.

Where was Megan? I'd tell her I had to go back and ask for her to tell Mrs Levine. Then I saw her and Jason climb the steps to the stage. There wasn't much time left. I decided to take a chance that no one would miss me. I dashed from the auditorium and down the hall to the classroom. I grabbed the music from my desk and zoomed back to the auditorium. I slid into my place beside Kim on the stage just as Mr Stickles picked up his baton and walked toward us. My heart thundered against my ribs. I took a deep breath and let it out slowly.

Mr Stickles had us sing all the songs before he announced the parts. Finally, clearing his throat, his huge Adam's apple bobbing in his throat, he said, "Rehearsal starts tomorrow, right after school. At that time, I'll give each of you a schedule. Remember, the success of the play doesn't depend on just the leading roles. It depends on all of us working together. OK now . . ."

My heart was beating so hard it roared in my ears and I could hardly hear what Mr Stickles said. As he named the flowers, the playing cards, Tweedledee and Tweedledum, and the March Hare the noise in the auditorium got louder and louder. Kids were squealing with excitement or moaning with disappointment and shuffling together in little groups. When he announced that Megan would be the Cheshire Cat, I sped to her side and gave her the high five.

"Quiet down, quiet down," Mr Stickles shouted. Then, when the racket had subsided to a few giggles, he continued, "White Rabbit, Jason Martinez; Queen of Hearts, Kim Sipes; and Alice, Kathy James."

My heart jumped and I squeezed my hands real tight. Megan hugged me and kept saying, "I knew you'd get Alice. I knew it." Then Jason was there, sticking his face between us and twitching his nose, just like a rabbit.

Kim, standing off by herself, shot me a murderous look. She'd never really been a friend. Now she was an enemy.

But I didn't care. I was Alice and, tonight, I'd write that letter to my mother.

Chapter Seven
Exciting News

"Wait, Kathy," Laurence called.

But I flew up the driveway. I couldn't wait to tell Mrs H. This morning, when I left, she said she'd keep her fingers crossed for me. Now she could uncross them. I was going to be Alice!

I pushed open the door and rushed into the warm porch room. "Mrs H! Mrs H!"

She came in from the spicy-smelling kitchen, holding flour-covered hands palms up. "You got it? You got the part?" she asked excitedly, her voice hoarse from a cold.

My face split into a smile. "I'm Alice, Alice in Wonderland."

Laurence pushed the door open, letting in a rush of cold air. "Can I go? Can I go to the play?" he piped.

Mrs H squeezed me in a big bear hug. For a minute, I relaxed against her pillowy chest. Then I pulled back.

Mrs H grabbed Laurence's and my hands and dragged us into a little circle dance. "Can I go? Can I go to the play?" asked Laurence again, pulling away and standing with his hands on his bony hips, his owl glasses a foggy grey.

"You sure can," said Mrs H. "We'll go to every performance. And we'll celebrate back here at the house afterwards. Jeremiah will want to come. And, Kathy, you can ask your friends." She pulled a tissue from a box on the counter and sneezed into it.

"Yippee!" shouted Laurence, throwing his coat on a chair and diving for Marmalade, who, as usual, was curled by the warm stove.

"Be extra gentle with her, Laurence. Marmalade got some exciting news today, too."

"What?" Laurence asked.

"I took her to the vet and found out she's going to have kittens."

Laurence gently stroked Marmalade, who meowed and stretched. "Kittens," he breathed. "Can I have one for my very own? Can I?"

"I think that might be arranged," Mrs H said.

He grinned up at me. "Did you hear that, Kathy? I'm going to have my own kitten."

I knelt down beside him and he scooted over to his Lego. I ran my hand over Marmalade's silky fur. "When is she going to have the kittens?"

"Sometime in May," Mrs H said.

I laid my cheek against Marmalade's purring belly. "May," I murmured. "That's when the play is. That's when my mother will come. I bet she likes kittens. I bet she'd let me take one with me."

Mrs H sat down in the chair near the window and, wide-eyed, gazed at me. "Kathy, what are you talking about?"

I looked at Bozo sitting on the windowsill behind Mrs H. I scrambled to my feet, took a deep breath and blurted, "Mrs H, I'll write to my mother and tell her about the play. Then she'll come to see me. She'll take me away with her. I'll be with my mother, my very own mother. I'll be where I belong."

Laurence jumped up from his Lego construction. "Kathy will be a star, just like her mother. Then her mother will love her."

Mrs H frowned at him, then turned to me. "Kathy, you don't even know where your mother is."

My stomach tightened into a ball. What if Mrs H wouldn't let my mother come? Could she stop her? "I do know where she is," I cried. "When I saw her on MTV, I wrote and got her address. I've been going to write to her ever since, but . . . well, now I really have something to write about. And if she can stay here . . . can she? Can my mother stay here when she comes to see me?"

A strange look came over Mrs H's face and her grey eyes lost their sparkle. She grabbed another tissue and blew her nose. "Well, Lordy," she sighed. "I didn't know you had your mother's address."

I stood still, holding my breath, waiting for her answer.

Her serious grey eyes met mine. "I thought you were settling in here, Kathy."

I twisted my hands tight and looked down. "I want to be with my mother. That's where I belong."

That night, sitting on my bed, Bozo on my lap, I finally wrote to my mother – the next step in my plan. And just in time, too. With luck, I'd be gone and living with her before Mrs H and Jeremiah Tyler announced their wedding plans. Over and over I wrote and crossed out. Finally, it was ready.

Dear Monica Starr James,

    I saw you on television and you were beautiful, just like I remember. I miss you very much. I'm going to be Alice in *Alice in Wonderland*. I'm going to sing just like you. Please come and see me in the play. Mrs H, that's the lady I'm living with, her name's really Mrs Hartwell. She said you could stay here with us. She said it would be fine.

    She lives at 10 Orchard Street, Middleboro, Connecticut. And her telephone number is 555-4321.

    The play is Saturday, May 15 at 4:00 and Sunday, May 16 at 2:00. Mrs H said you could stay overnight. You can have my room. Please come. I miss you.

Love from Kathy
your daughter.

P.S. I'm very grown up and take care of myself now. I'm not any work. And I can stay alone. I even stay alone in the house and watch Laurence sometimes.

I checked the letter for the umpteenth time. Almost perfect. I'd been sitting so long, my legs were stiff. I stretched and went to the window, and pressed my forehead and palms against the cold pane.

Beyond the stone wall, the black skeleton limbs of the apple trees moved in the moonlight. My apple tree, the one that stood alone near the wall, creaked up and down sadly. It didn't look like it would ever be beautiful, like Mrs Cruz said. I pulled the shade against the shivery night.

I unbuttoned my navy blouse, tossed it on the bed and reached for my pyjamas under the pillow. There on the back of the blouse were two white smudges, flour from Mrs H's hands.

I'd felt so safe circled in her big hug. I thought of her smiling eyes, then of how the smile went out of them when I told her about my plan, and the funny look on her face. That look – why? Had I hurt her feelings when I told her I wanted to go with my mother? I couldn't remember ever hurting anyone's feelings before. It made me feel kind of sad, but kind of good, too.

Chapter Eight
The Accusation

The mailbox lid clanged shut. I stared at it, trying to imagine my mother's face when she opened the letter. But all I could see was her dancing slowly away from me. I couldn't catch hold of her – like in my dream.

Walking through a cold grey mist up the driveway, the world seemed unreal, like my mother's TV image. Through the window, I could see Bozo sitting on the sill. Seeing him made my mother more real. I could almost smell her perfume, hear her sing a snatch of song. My breath caught in my throat. I needed my mother. She would come. She had to come.

I stepped into the warm house and everything seemed bright and clear. Mrs H was tossing a log into the stove. Marmalade, forced to move, watched her, then picked her way through the Lego structures. She looked like a huge giant in a small world, but she was so graceful, she disturbed only a few dust balls.

"Hurry up," I called to Laurence, who still dawdled over breakfast. "The bus will be here soon." I tingled with excitement. Today, rehearsals started. Today, my plan really got going. And Laurence was still eating breakfast!

Finally, we left the house. Then, hurrying down the icy drive, Laurence slipped and fell into a slushy puddle. "Now look what you've done," I cried, helping him to his feet. "You're soaking wet. We'll miss the bus for sure." Fifteen minutes later, Mrs H drove us to school.

I could hear the hubbub of voices through the classroom door as I hung my jacket on a wall hook. When I opened the door, everyone stopped talking and stared at me. What was going on? Other kids were late sometimes, but nobody stared at them when they came in.

Kim tossed her head and pursed her lips. Narrowing her blue eyes, she glared at me. "There she is now. I'm surprised she has the nerve to come to school."

I froze in the doorway.

"Kathy, take your seat," Mrs Levine ordered, her voice sharp.

Kim jumped to her feet. "I know she took it, Mrs Levine. When she came back to music she was all out of breath and she had something all bunched up in her pocket. I bet she took it for her mother, her *famous* TV mother." The hate in her voice exploded against me.

Mrs Levine frowned. "Kim, sit down. That's enough. I'll talk to both you and Kathy later."

My voice burst from my throat. "Took what? What is she talking about?"

"You know you took Mrs Levine's watch. That's why you disappeared just before music," Kim shouted.

My stomach squeezed tight and rose to my throat. "Her watch? The one that fell off the chain? Mrs Levine put it in her pocket."

Tommy Perkins, sitting behind Kim, pointed a pencil at me. "In her sweater pocket. And she left her sweater in the classroom."

Bubbles of anger stirred in me. Tommy believed that witch, Kim. How many of the other kids believed her? Mrs Levine? Did she believe her, too?

I looked over at Megan. Her face as red as her hair, she bent her head and wiped her eyes with the back of her hand. Did she believe Kim, too?

"I don't care what any of you think," I screamed, and tore from the room.

Halfway down the hall, I ran smack into Mr Stickles.

"Whoa there," he said, grabbing my arms with long, bony fingers. "Where's the fire?"

"Let me go," I shouted. "You won't believe me either. Nobody ever believes me." I wrenched myself free and flew down the hall.

Outside, a mix of rain and snow swirled before my eyes and cooled my burning face. I ran through the wet car park, my legs heavy, as though I were running through water. But I surged on, down the winding road, till the pain in my side stopped me. Leaning against a telephone pole, I gasped for breath. Anger boiled inside me. It wasn't fair!

I trudged down the road toward home. Not home really – to Mrs H's house. Then I stopped and just stood there, shivering. The icy rain plastered my sweater and jeans against me. I didn't want to go to Mrs H's. Where could I go? If only I could go to my mother. She would know what to do.

I pressed my hands against my dripping hair. My mother! I'd mailed the letter this morning. Now I wouldn't be in the play. And it was all Kim's fault. They'd give her the part of Alice. I hated her!

Brakes squealed and Mrs H's orange VW stalled

across the street. "Kathy," she croaked, her voice hoarser than yesterday, "come get in out of the rain."

"No," I shouted, starting back up the hill.

"Kathy James, you get in this car right now."

Something in her tone made me turn around. I stood there, rain running down my face, staring at her. Then, I crossed the street and climbed in beside her.

I sat, dripping wet, in stony silence, wrapping the anger inside myself. Mrs H turned the key on, then off, all the while pushing at the pedals. Finally, the motor chugged to life and the car lurched forward.

She didn't say a word until we pulled into the driveway. Then, "Mrs Levine called. She was worried about you."

"Yeah, sure," I muttered.

"Kathy, I . . ."

Here it comes, I thought. First, I can't believe you'd steal. Then, why, Kathy? I've been trying so hard with you. Blah. Blah. Blah. Well, I didn't want to hear it.

I slammed out of the car into a fierce blast of icy rain.

Chapter Nine
The Blow-Up

A hot ball boiled in my stomach and burst through me. I'd lost everything! The chance to be in the play. The chance to be with my mother.

I banged into the porch room. The wind battered the door behind me. I pressed my hands against my head to stop the roaring. My foot lashed out and smashed into Laurence's kingdom. Again and again I kicked the plastic blocks. Picked them up, tore them apart. Throwing. Stomping. Screaming.

Mrs H's voice seemed to come from far away. "Kathy! Kathy! Stop it!"

She reached for me.

I pulled away, my arms flailing out, hitting her.

I grabbed a tower, wrenched it apart. Pointed edges of the Lego stabbed my palms. The pain pierced my rage.

I crumpled to the floor and buried my face in my hands, rocking back and forth.

I felt lighter.

Empty.

Terrified.

Mrs H knelt beside me and put her arm around my shoulders. I longed to lean against her and cry, but I couldn't. I knew she must hate me. I jerked away. "Leave me alone. I don't want you."

She pulled back and all the light went from her grey eyes.

A surge of power swept through me. I could hurt somebody. Me. Good!

Mrs H stood up slowly and wiped her hand across her face. Horrified, I watched a tiny stream of blood trickle from her nose and wet her upper lip. Had I done that? Had I made her bleed?

She looked down at the shattered plastic. "Poor Laurence. He'll be devastated. All his work."

An image of Laurence snuggling against Mrs H while she read to him filled my head, and I was glad – glad that I'd ruined his old Lego. I stood up and hugged my arms to my chest to stop the trembling. "He won't care. He has you, his mother. When I leave, he'll have you all to himself."

"Leave? Oh, Kathy." Mrs H sat down on the sagging plaid couch, the destroyed Lego scattered about her feet. She pulled some tissues from her pocket and blew her nose, then patted the cushion next to her. "Sit down, Kathy. We need to talk."

I slitted my eyes and stared at her, swallowing back the tears that threatened to choke me. Here it comes. She's going to call Mrs Cruz. She's going to send me away.

Panic knotted my stomach. Mrs H didn't want me and I wasn't going to be in the play. What if my mother didn't come? Well, I didn't care. "I can take care of myself," I said, my voice sounding tight and funny.

"Kathy, I don't want you to leave. I want you to stay here. You shouldn't have done this," she said, looking at the mess on the floor and shaking her head. "You'll have to apologize to Laurence, make it up to him somehow. But I don't want you to leave."

Her words bounced against me, not sinking in. "Wh . . . what do you mean?" I stammered.

"I mean I want you to stay here with Laurence and me."

"You're not going to send me back?"

"Oh, Kathy." Mrs H's big smile spread over her face and her eyes lit up. "I'd never send you back. I don't know if this is the time to tell you, but . . . I think you should know. And maybe now is the time. I've been talking to Mrs Cruz about keeping you – adopting you."

"Adopt . . . adopting me?"

"Yes. Then I'd be your mother, too. Just like Laurence's."

I looked down and toed a few Lego. "I have a mother. I won't be in the play now, but . . . maybe . . . maybe she'll come anyway. When she gets the letter, she'll want me with her."

Mrs H didn't answer.

"It's true," I said, my voice rising. "I'm older and not so much work. And I won't lose my temper, not ever again."

Mrs H stood up and put her hands on my shoulders. "We'll talk about all that later. You're shivering and your teeth are chattering. Upstairs with you now. Off with those wet clothes, into a hot bath, then lunch."

Soaking in the hot tub, I thought about what Mrs H had said. She couldn't really want me, not after what I'd done to Laurence's Lego. Anyway, Mr Tyler didn't want me. For sure! And I didn't want them. I wanted my mother, my own mother.

At lunch, I was toying with my food, wondering

how I could ever go back to school when the phone rang. Mrs H picked it up, then kept nodding her head and saying, "I see." Every so often, she'd look at me. Finally, she hung up and smiled. "That was Mrs Levine. She wanted to tell you that they know who took her watch, and . . ."

"Who? Who took it?"

"She didn't say, but she did say she never thought it was you."

Blood rushed to my face. "That's what she says now. But I bet she did think I took it. I bet you did, too."

Mrs H's eyebrows shot up. "Why do you say that?"

I looked away. "I just know it."

"Well, you're wrong. I thought no such thing. Kathy, give people a chance."

I remembered Mrs Cruz saying, *"Give Mrs H a chance."* Could I be wrong? Does Mrs H really trust me?

Suddenly everything seemed brighter. "What . . . what about the play?" I asked.

"Mr Stickles expects you there this afternoon for rehearsals."

Relief flowed through me. I was going to be in the play after all. My plan could go ahead. My mother would come.

Chapter Ten
Exposed

When I walked into the auditorium, I saw Mr Stickles, skeleton-thin, hunched over a table, sorting a stack of papers. I blushed, thinking of how I'd run from him that morning.

He turned and grinned at me. "Hey, Kathy, how's the sprinter? Come on down here and help me sort these schedules out. Here's yours," he said, handing me the script and two pages stapled together. "You have lots of lines to learn. We'll be here many an hour. But, come May, it will be worth it."

My stomach tumbled with excitement. I remembered the day I'd overheard Kim say I'd never get the part, that I was too quiet. But when I was on stage, it was like I became somebody else. I turned the pages of the script carefully. Oh, how I hoped I'd be a good Alice. My mother just had to be proud of me.

The auditorium doors swung open and the other kids burst in. When Megan saw me, she ran down the aisle and grabbed my shoulders. "Can you believe it?" she squealed. "What a snake Kim Sipes is!"

Her fingers dug into my arms. I wriggled away. "That's for sure," I agreed.

She jumped up and down, her red hair bobbing about her face. "You don't know the half of it. Kim took the watch. Tommy Perkins squealed on her."

My heart shot into my throat. "Kim took the watch? And said I did?"

"That's right."

My hands tightened on the script. "How could she?"

"She must have been furious when you got Alice. She took the watch when she got back to the classroom. Tommy saw her. I guess he felt bad after you ran out this morning, and he squealed on her!"

My face flamed with anger and my voice choked. "I'll never speak to her again. She almost made me miss being in the play!"

"Now she's not going to be in the play. Serves her right. What a day! I wondered what happened to you. You should have come back. Kim burst out crying when Tommy told. Then Mrs Levine took her to the office. You missed all the excitement!"

Suddenly, a whisper went through the auditorium. Then it got quiet.

Megan caught back a little cry. "Look! There's Kim with Mrs Levine."

Kim, her cheeks two bright apples, walked down the aisle straight towards me. Mrs Levine waited by the doors.

Kim glared at me, then, in a voice loud enough for Mrs Levine to hear, said, "I'm sorry I accused you of taking the watch." She spun away and walked over to Mr Stickles.

Megan sniffed. "Some apology. I felt so bad for you this morning. I was practically in tears. I just knew you didn't take Mrs Levine's watch. I've wondered all day if you'd show up for rehearsals. Where did you go this morning?"

"I'll tell you later," I promised, a warm glow at her trust spreading through me. "Guess what! I wrote to my mother telling her when the play is."

"Oh wow! I can't wait to meet her. Just think, a television star right here at Middleboro Elementary," Megan gushed. She ran her hands through her mop of hair and opened her eyes wide. "I'll be nervous as heck up on stage in front of her."

"You? How about me? What if I'm a flop? What if my voice squeaks?"

"You won't be a flop. And you've got a fantastic voice. You'll . . ."

"Kathy," Mrs H called. She and Laurence were walking down the aisle towards me. Laurence sprinted ahead. "Can I watch rehearsals, Kathy? Can I?" he asked, hopping from foot to foot. I could tell Mrs H hadn't told him about the Lego yet.

"Not today, Laurence," said Mrs H, joining us. "I've got to take care of this cold, Kathy, so Jeremiah's going to pick you up after rehearsal."

I watched them walk back up the aisle. Halfway up, Laurence turned to wave. My heart sank. I waved back. He'd worked so hard on his kingdom.

Kim's sarcastic voice broke into my thoughts. "Is Mrs Hartwell the lady you're staying with? Is she your mother's friend?"

"What do you care?"

"Everyone knows Mrs Hartwell takes in foster-children – kids whose parents don't want them. That's how she makes money, you know. She gets paid for taking care of them . . . of you."

My heart started to pound. This couldn't be happening. I wished I could shrink and disappear. I'd been here less than two months and no one knew I was a foster-child. Mrs Levine had never told. Why did Mrs

H have to come in here and ruin everything? "You don't know what you're talking about," I said, my mouth dry.

"Oh, yes, I do. Once she had a retard that probably ended up in an institution. And last year she had some weirdo girl. Now she's got you."

"Shut up," I hissed.

"Tell her, Megan," Kim commanded in a cool voice.

"Get lost, Kim," said Megan, her eyes flashing. "Come on, Kathy. Mr Stickles wants us on stage."

"You don't have a mother, do you? All this stuff about her being on television is just a bunch of lies," Kim gloated.

"Oh, no, it isn't," I flared. "I have a mother and she's coming to see me be Alice. Then I'm going to live with her."

I followed Megan on to the stage, my heart hammering. My mother would come. She had to.

"Well, Kathy, how did the rehearsal go?" Mr Tyler asked as he pulled out of the car park. "OK," I mumbled.

"Umm. That's good." We drove along in silence for a while, a brisk wind rattling his old van. Then he said, "Nasty cold Pat's got. She's got to take better care of

67

herself. Works too hard. Has too much to do. Baking. Taking care of Laurence and you."

Suddenly I was six years old, back in Mrs Cruz's office hearing my mother say, *"I just can't take care of myself and a kid too. It's impossible."*

Mr Tyler's voice, slowed by his laboured breathing, lectured on. "Now that you're in this play, I hope you'll still help out with the baking. Pat's just got too much to do."

Anger prickled through me. I was tired of his criticising me all the time. "I do help," I snapped. "But don't worry, I'll be out of here by early summer, then you and Mrs H can get married."

Mr Tyler's head swivelled and, round-eyed, he stared at me. "Married?" The van swerved and an oncoming car blasted its horn. Mr Tyler jerked the wheel round and looked back at the road. "Did you say 'married'?"

"Yes, married. Laurence told me. He heard you and Mrs H talking."

A low, rumbling laugh started in Mr Tyler's big stomach, then burst out his mouth. He laughed and laughed, making the seat jiggle. After a moment, he reached into his pocket and pulled out a huge white handkerchief, wiped his eyes and blew his nose.

I looked at him, stunned. "What's so funny?"

"Oh, Kathy," he chuckled, reaching over and patting my shoulder. "Why would Pat want to marry an old man with a bad ticker like me?"

"But you're always getting together. You're always talking, and Laurence said you're going to Florida on your honeymoon. He said you were going to be his father. That you'd be a real family."

Suddenly sombre, Mr Tyler said, "Oh, dear! Pat and I have some clearing up to do. I am going to Florida, but Pat isn't. You see, I'm retiring, selling my share of the Coffee Stop to Pat and moving to the sunny south. Doctor's orders."

"Retiring? Then you and Mrs H aren't getting married?" I asked, my voice rising.

"No, we're not getting married." He laughed a little. "You don't have to look so relieved. Guess you don't like me much, eh?"

I didn't say anything. Just turned and looked out the window.

"I bet you think I'm a bossy old man, always telling you what to do. It's just that I'm worried about Pat. She's going to be sole owner of the Coffee Stop. I hope it isn't going to be too much for her."

The van pulled into the driveway and braked to a stop. I opened the door and hopped down.

"Kathy, leave it to Pat and me to explain to Laurence." Mr Tyler rubbed his chin. "We'd better do it soon, tomorrow."

"OK," I said. "Thanks for the ride."

His voice stopped me. "But I've got some good news. You tell him Maisie's going to have kittens, too."

I watched the van pull away. Cold air whistled down my jacket collar. The smell of wood smoke made me long for the cosy porch room. But I hated to go in and face Laurence. I'd destroyed his kingdom, and tomorrow, Mrs H and Mr Tyler would destroy his dream of a real family. I gazed up at the sky. The wind had blown the clouds away, leaving it a clear, navy blue. I searched for a star and murmured, "Star light, star bright, the first star I see tonight, I wish I may I wish I might have the wish I wish tonight." I squeezed my eyes tight and wished – hoped – that Laurence wouldn't be too mad at me.

I pushed the door open and stepped into the warm porch room. It was eerily quiet. No Laurence clicking Lego together. No Mrs H rattling pots and pans in the kitchen. The Lego canisters were neatly stacked where

I'd left them. The kitchen was tidy and clean, smelling of cinnamon and apples. The only thing that seemed the same was Marmalade, curled by the glowing stove.

I heard Mrs H's heavy step on the stairs. She walked through the dining-room into the kitchen. "Hi, Kathy," she said, her voice a raspy whisper. "I've got your supper ready to warm up." She started pulling dishes out of the refrigerator.

My stomach churned as I hung up my jacket. "Where's Laurence?" I asked.

Mrs H spooned macaroni and cheese into a bowl. After a time, she said, "He had an early supper and went early to bed."

A hard lump settled in my centre. "What . . . what did he say about . . . you know . . .?"

Mrs H left the macaroni and bowl and sat down in one of the straight-backed kitchen chairs. "Well, Kathy, he was very upset. You can just imagine. And . . . well, he didn't think before he acted. Oh, dear, I don't know how to tell you."

The back of my neck prickled. "Tell me what?"

"I know he's sorry about it, just like you're sorry about busting up his Lego."

"What did he do?" I asked, my breath coming faster. I followed her eyes to the windowsill where Bozo always waited for me.

"Bozo," I whispered.

"I'm sorry, Kathy. And so is Laurence. Really sorry."

"Bozo. Where is he?"

Mrs H pushed back her chair and moved towards me. "Laurence acted on impulse, Kathy. You had hurt him and he wanted to hurt you. Without thinking, he grabbed Bozo and . . . before I could even move, he . . . he threw him into the stove."

Icy shivers darted through me. "He burned him? He burned him? Mommy gave him to me for Christmas."

"I know how much Bozo meant to you," Mrs H said, reaching out to me.

I lunged towards the dining-room. "And now he's hiding in his room? Just wait till I . . ."

Mrs H moved fast and seized my arms. "Kathy, don't go up. Wait till tomorrow. It will be better if you talk tomorrow."

"Don't touch me," I screamed. "All you care about is Laurence. I'm just a weirdo foster-kid you get money for."

I flew up the stairs to my bedroom, blocking out the look on Mrs H's face.

Chapter Eleven
Aftermath

I curled into a shatterproof ball on my bed, squeezing my eyes so tight lights flashed behind my eyelids. My throat swelled with unshed tears. I huddled there wondering if my pounding heart would burst through my chest, if the dizzying roar in my ears would ever stop.

Hours later, I woke cramped and confused. Why was I lying on top of the covers with an afghan over me? Why did I have this ache in my chest? I reached for Bozo.

Then I remembered.

A shuddery breath shivered through me. I swung my legs over the edge of the bed. My feet touched the cold wood floor. I opened the window and a fresh breeze brushed my hot face. I drew in a deep breath, tasting snow in the air. I knelt there, pulling the afghan tight around my shoulders. Mrs H must have come in and covered me. That business about adopting me – did she mean it? Even if she did, she'd change her mind after tonight. Two wild outbursts! She'd send me away for sure, just like everybody else.

A few stars lit the sky. The bare limbs of my apple tree reached out to the night as though searching for something. It looked lonelier than ever. I thought of my wish. I'd felt so sorry for Laurence, sorry that I'd smashed his Lego, sorry for his disappointment when Mrs H and Mr Tyler talk to him. Now look what he'd done. I hated him!

Bozo. I felt like part of my mother had died. But . . . my mother was still alive. I had her address and I'd just written to her. That morning. It seemed like years and years ago. Oh, I hope she writes or calls soon. She just has to come to the play. And then . . . But I couldn't think past then. I closed the window and stood up. My feet were blocks of ice. Shivering, I slid between the cold sheets, the afghan still wrapped round me.

The next morning, my legs and arms felt heavy. I didn't want to get out of bed and face Mrs H and Laurence. Things had been OK till yesterday. Then Kim had accused me of being a thief, and had found out that I was a foster-child. I hated her! And Bozo . . . poor Bozo! I hated Laurence, too!

I stood in front of the mirror, yanking a brush through my tangled hair. I heard a soft knock on the door, then Laurence's voice, "Kathy, can I come in?"

"Go away."

"Please, Kathy." The door opened and there was Laurence, bruise-like shadows showing under the rims of his glasses. "I'm sorry about Bozo," he mumbled, bowing his head so I couldn't see his face.

"Yeah, I bet," I said, surprised at a sudden impulse to tell him I was sorry about the Lego. Why should I care about him after what he'd done to Bozo? And he didn't even want me here. He'd made that clear from the very beginning.

"You didn't have to ruin my kingdom," he burst out.

I slammed down the brush and, holding on to my anger, narrowed my eyes. "You can always build it again, can't you? But Bozo's gone. You burned him," I hissed.

He stood there in his blue pyjamas patterned with red and yellow race cars, twisting his thin hands together. "I'm sorry, Kathy. I wish I hadn't done it."

I tightened my grip on the brush. "If you're really, truly sorry, there's only one way to prove it."

"How?"

"Never ever build with your Lego again."

For a moment, he didn't say a word. He just stood

there, the light from the window glinting off his round glasses. Then, slowly crossing his heart, he said, "Cross my heart and hope to die, I'll never build with my Lego again."

"Yeah, I bet! You'll never keep your promise."

"Yes, I will. I'm really, really sorry about Bozo."

Bozo – tossed into that hot fire!

Bozo. Red-hot anger shuddered through me again. Wanting to hurt Laurence as much as he'd hurt me, I shouted, "Your mother and Mr Tyler aren't getting married. Mr Tyler told me so last night."

Laurence stood absolutely still. The blood drained from his face. His eyes widened and his mouth fell open. Finally, he managed to say, "You're just saying that to be mean."

"It's true. Ask your mother."

Laurence turned, tore out of the room and thundered down the stairs, shouting, "Mommy! Mommy!"

I loosened my grip on the brush I'd been squeezing and turning in my hands so hard the bristles had dug into my palms. I didn't feel any better. Bozo was still gone.

After that, there was a kind of truce in the house. I ignored Laurence and he ignored me. At first, when I came home from rehearsals, I wondered why the porch room seemed so big, so quiet. Then I realised – there was no more click-clicking of Lego being stuck together, no more murmur of Laurence's voice as he spun stories. The big canisters weren't even in sight. They had disappeared as completely as Bozo. Once, Mrs H suggested that I tell Laurence to go ahead and build with his Lego, but I just turned away from her.

One rainy April day, when I didn't have rehearsals, I opened the door to the delicious smell of hot blueberry pie. Mrs H had just slid the pie on to a cooling rack, but the pie slid right off. She saved the hot dish from crashing to the floor with her bare hands.

"Ow!" she cried. She sucked on her fingers, then peered at them. "Look at that, a blister. And I still have all the muffins to do."

I hesitated. I hadn't helped in the kitchen for a long time. "Ah, I'll make them," I offered.

"That would be a big help, Kathy," she said, holding her hand under cold water. "You don't want to lose your touch. You do make nice fluffy muffins."

I set out all the ingredients I needed – milk, oil, flour, sugar, baking powder, baking soda, salt, and carrots. I was careful not to scrape my knuckles as I grated the carrots, knowing that in the past I'd added a little skin to them. I giggled.

Mrs H pulled a rubber glove over her bandaged hand to wash dishes. "What's tickled your funny bone?" she asked.

"I was just thinking that the people who ate the muffins that had a little skinned knuckle in them were cannibals."

Mrs H threw back her head and dissolved into laughter. I smiled. I liked making Mrs H laugh.

Marmalade wandered into the kitchen, meowed loudly as though scolding us, then, tail high, disappeared into the dining-room.

Mrs H made little clucking noises. "Feeling peevish, Marmalade, what with all those kitties growing inside you?"

"How many do you think she'll have?"

"Could be as many as eight. But I hope it's only two or three. Kathy?" she said, in a funny kind of voice.

"What?" I asked, looking at her. Her clear grey eyes held mine. "Remember when I told you I'd like to adopt you?"

I nodded.

"Well, that still goes. You think about it. You give me the word and I'll tell Mrs Cruz to start the legal proceedings."

I took the cover off the flour canister and picked up

a measuring cup. "But . . . my mother. She'll come to the play, and then . . . why then, she'll want me to go with her."

"Kathy . . . don't get your hopes up too high on that."

Concentrating, I spooned flour into the cup, thinking of Mrs Cruz. A few weeks ago she had visited and, her big, dark eyes popping, had leaned toward me and said, "Kathy, you must let go of this fantasy you have. Don't you see what you have right here? Pat Hartwell loves you. She's the one who's your mother. You just don't realise it."

Keeping my eyes on the measuring cup, I said, "You sound just like Mrs Cruz. She always makes it sound like my mother doesn't want me. But I know she does. I know she wants me just as much as I want her."

"Well, you just remember you've always got a home here, OK?"

I nodded. I wanted to hug her, to lay my head on her chest, but I didn't dare. Did she really want me here for always or would she send me away some day? Anyway, I had promised Laurence I'd be gone by June. He certainly didn't want me around. And, soon, any minute, I'd hear from my mother.

Chapter Twelve
Another Foster Mother

"I'm late; I'm late; I'm in a rabbit stew . . ." Jason chanted as he slid his tray on the table, splashing the soup.

"If you were in a stew, it would disappear pronto. I never saw anybody eat as much as you," said Megan, biting into her sandwich.

It was Monday, May 8th, and ever since play rehearsals had started, Jason was forever humming, singing, or shouting, "I'm late; I'm late."

Kim sauntered over and stood at the end of the table. She smoothed her shiny black hair with her hands and stared at me with round blue eyes. "The play's this Saturday. I'm curious and curiouser, Kathy, just like Alice. Have you heard from your *wonderfully* famous mother yet?"

My throat felt dry and I could hardly swallow my

bite of tuna sandwich. Every day, since I'd mailed the letter, I couldn't wait to get home to see if I had a letter or a phone call from my mother. Here it was, the week of the play, and nothing.

Before I could say anything, Megan, green eyes flashing, said, "How about *your* grandparents? Are they coming to see you sitting in the audience? Anyway, Kathy's mother is a movie star. Movie stars are busy people."

Kim glowered. "A movie star? Some bit piece on television. My mother says that doesn't make her a movie star."

A cold lump formed in my stomach. "She is so a movie star. And she's a wonderful singer."

"Um. But you haven't heard from her, right? You might as well admit it, Kathy. Your mother isn't coming. She deserted you. She doesn't want you."

I jumped up and my chair toppled over. "Shut up, Kim. Shut up!"

"Cool it, Kim," Megan warned.

"I was just curious," Kim said, strolling away. Jason sliced the air with his knife. "Off with her head!"

Megan leaned across the table. "Don't pay any attention to her, Kathy. She's just jealous because you got the lead and now she's not even in the play."

"And she's mad 'cause she got detention for taking the watch. Every night for two weeks," Jason muttered around a mouthful of food.

"Serves her right," Megan said, her fair skin flushing. "It should have been longer."

Jason and Megan were real friends. I sat down, my rapid heartbeat slowing a little. "You know, I bet I'll hear from my mother today."

Later, walking up the driveway to the house, Laurence dawdling behind me, the words from one of Alice's songs kept running through my head – "Be patient is very good advice." But I'd been patient so long. I stopped and looked up at the budding apple tree. Maybe today was the day. Maybe today there would be a letter.

I pushed open the door and looked at the end table where Mrs H put the mail. Nothing. That familiar heavy feeling settled in my chest.

The house seemed quiet. A rolled-out piecrust lay on the counter. Where could Mrs H be? Just then, her finger to her lips, she tiptoed in from the dining-room. "Kathy, Laurence," she whispered, as Laurence came in. "Come quick. Marmalade's had two kittens and I think another's on the way."

We dropped our books on the table and followed her to the second parlour. This sure was kitten week. Maisie, Mr Tyler's cat, had had eight kittens yesterday. When we got to the second parlour, we were just in time to see a kitten slide out from under Marmalade's tail on to her old sleeping quilt.

Laurence, his eyes huge behind his glasses, said, "It looks like a mouse. And it's all wet and messy. Its eyes aren't even open."

"Watch how Marmalade cleans it up," said Mrs H.

Marmalade licked the tiny animal until we could see its black-and-white fur. Then she bit a long cord that came from the kitten's belly.

"What's that thing? Why is Marmalade eating it?" asked Laurence in a whisper.

Mrs H chuckled. "That's the umbilical cord. That's how the kittens get their nourishment while they're growing inside their mother. And Marmalade's not eating it. She's biting it in two. The kittens don't need it any more. Now they can live on their own."

"How does Marmalade know she should bite the cord?" I wondered.

"Instinct, Kathy. Marmalade's a good mother. See. Now that she's cleaned herself up, she'll let her kittens nurse."

"I want the black-and-white one," said Laurence, pointing.

I watched the three kittens – one black, one black-and-white, and one orange – attach themselves to Marmalade's nipples. They were so tiny. They couldn't live without their mother. What was it like for human mothers to have babies? My mother must have loved me when I was born, just like Marmalade loved her babies.

Our heads turned at the squeak of the kitchen door.

"Must be Jeremiah," said Mrs H. "He's bringing over one of Maisie's kittens . . . "

"How come?" I asked.

"She refuses to feed him. He was the last one born and he's the runt of the litter."

Mr Tyler, holding a lumpy face-cloth against his chest, lumbered in.

"Let's see the little guy," said Mrs H, pulling apart the corners of the face-cloth.

"He's trembling," said Mr Tyler. "I tried and tried to get Maisie to nurse him, but . . ."

"Can I hold him?" I asked, reaching out my hands.

"He shouldn't be handled too much," said Mr Tyler.

I dropped my hands.

"It's OK, Jeremiah," said Mrs H, taking the kitten from him and placing it in my hands. His little grey body was warm and almost weightless. I could feel the tiny bones beneath his skin.

"Put him on the quilt where the kittens were born. Then he'll smell like Marmalade's kittens," Mr Tyler suggested.

I set him down on his feet. He staggered and fell. I wrapped some of the cloth around him, rubbing the moisture gently into his grey coat. Marmalade sniffed him when I placed him in front of her. She looked up at me, meowed, sniffed him again, then started licking him. I let out a deep breath I didn't realise I'd been holding. The kitten crawled to Marmalade's belly, pushed between the orange and black kittens and latched on to a nipple.

Mr Tyler grinned and his bushy eyebrows wriggled. "Looks like it's going to work, eh, Kathy?" he said, rocking back on his heels.

"Yep, kitten's got a new mommy," said Mrs H, chuckling and wiping her eyes.

"He's got a foster-mother," said Laurence, leaning against Mrs H. "Like me and Kathy got you."

Chapter Thirteen
The Phone Call

"You mean like me," I said, gazing at the kittens nuzzling against Marmalade. "Mrs H is your real mother, like Marmalade is to her own three babies."

"No, sir, I didn't always live here, did I, Mommy?"

"I thought you knew that, Kathy," said Mrs H. "Laurence came to my husband and me as a foster-child, then we adopted him like I want . . . ."

The phone jangled in the kitchen. For a moment no one answered it, then Mr Tyler said, "I'll get it."

I couldn't believe it. All this time I'd thought Laurence was Mrs H's own son. I looked at the grey kitten, a curled sleeping ball. He looked like he belonged, just like the other kittens. Would Marmalade treat him differently?

Mr Tyler, his eyebrows raised high, clumped back into the room. "Kathy, phone's for you. Some woman says she's your mother."

I caught my breath, then walked slowly to the kitchen, my heart pounding. What would I say? I picked up the phone. "Hello," my voice squeaked. I cleared my throat and tried again. "Hello."

A hurried, breathless voice on the other end of the phone. Hearing it brought a rush of memories: *Frantic packing. Icy streets. Bozo. Mrs Cruz. A promise – "I'll come back."*

And now she had come back! She had kept her promise! My chest swelled with happiness.

"Kathy, are you there? For heaven's sake, you're so quiet. Aren't you glad to hear from me?" said the faraway voice.

My heart, hammering in my ears, made it hard to hear. "Yes. Yes. Did you get my letter? You looked so beautiful on TV."

"Oh, that old video. I'm on to better prospects now. Jim has some good connections. I'll make it big yet. Just you wait and see."

"Jim?"

"He's my latest. Listen, sweetie, we'll be in Connecticut Saturday, so we'll stop by for the show."

"You will? You're really going to come?"

"Kathy, are you dense or what? What did I just say?"

"Mrs H said you could stay here. Then we can make plans."

"I'll check with Jim. Can you give me directions?"

"Just a minute. I'll get Mrs H." I dashed into the back parlour. "Mrs H, it's my mother. She needs directions."

I stood nearby, hardly breathing while Mrs H talked. The kitchen clock ticked louder than I'd ever heard it, and the smell of overripe bananas filled the room. "She's coming, she's coming" sang through my head. "Let me say goodbye," I said, reaching for the phone.

"Kathy wants to say goodbye . . . hello, hello." Mrs H hung up the phone. "She didn't hear me, Kathy."

My heart sank. "Oh," I whispered. Then a surge of happiness swept me off my feet, and I twirled around, hugging myself. "She's coming, Mrs H. She's really coming."

"Yes, she is." Mrs H smiled but her eyes looked kind of sad.

"Did she say what time?"

"Just that she and her friend, Jim, would be here mid-morning Saturday."

A shadow, like a cloud on a sunny day. Why did Jim have to come? But then, a great burst of joy – my mother was coming back!

Saturday. Only five more days! Just wait till I tell Megan! Just wait till Kim hears!

The week dragged by even though we had rehearsals every afternoon. Finally, it was Thursday; two more days. Laurence and I got off the bus and started up the long driveway. Laurence had never mentioned the Lego since that horrible day. Never mentioned that Mrs H and Mr Tyler weren't getting married. Instead of building with his Lego he spent lots of time drawing and colouring. The kitchen and porch room were now full of his artwork.

"I'm going to call my kitten Skunky," he said.

"Skunky? That's a terrible name. I thought you said Fluffy."

"But she's black-and-white. She looks like a skunk."

"Better hope she doesn't smell like one."

He giggled. "What are you going to name your kitten?"

"Foster."

"Foster? Oh, I get it. 'Cause he's a foster-kitten." He pulled on my sleeve and turned to face me. "Kathy?"

"What?" I asked, shifting my books from one arm to the other.

Staring at me through his big glasses he said, "Remember the promise you made me?"

"You mean about leaving by June?"

He nodded.

I walked faster to get away from him, surprised that his words hurt. "Don't worry about it. My plan's working. Didn't I tell you I'd get the part of Alice? Didn't I tell you my mother would come?"

"Wait, Kathy. Don't get mad. I . . . I just wondered. What if you can't go with your mother?"

I stopped and glared at him. "I can. Who's going to stop me?"

His thin little face looked very serious. "Well . . . I mean . . . I thought Mommy and Uncle Jerry . . . you know."

I slid a glance at him. "Look, Laurence," I mumbled. "I'm sorry I told you. I should have let Mrs H and Mr Tyler tell you."

Laurence bit his lower lip and nodded his head. "But, Kathy, what if your mother doesn't want you?"

"She wants me, Laurence. She's coming back like she promised she would. And I'll leave, just like I promised you."

"Well . . . I don't want you to leave, Kathy. I want you to stay." His face flaming, he sprinted ahead of me and dashed into the house.

I stared after him, then set my books on the back step. I jumped over the upturned earth Mrs H had prepared for flowers, and climbed the stone stairs to the upper yard.

The once bare branches of my apple tree were heavy with green buds that glistened in the afternoon sun. I fit my bottom between two roots of the tree and leaned against its rough bark. A happy little feeling settled in my stomach. Laurence wanted me to stay. He didn't want me to leave. Maybe it was the kittens. I'd felt closer to him since they were born. They were so fragile. We couldn't touch them much because Marmalade got mad. She'd pick them up by the neck and hide them. I watched her closely. She treated the grey kitten just like the others. Didn't she know it wasn't hers? Or didn't she care?

I twirled a twig round and round. Foster – so tiny and soft. I'd looked up "foster" and "parent" in the dictionary. It said to foster was to bring up, to nurture, to cherish, and that a parent was one who gives birth to, or nurtures and raises a child. I guess that made Marmalade Foster's mother and Mrs H Laurence's.

Mrs H. She'd been kind of quiet since my mother called. I guess because of me. But I'd told her I'd be leaving. I'd told her my mother would come. Did she really care? After all, all my other foster-parents had been glad to get rid of me. But Mrs H wasn't like the others.

Mrs H opened the door and called, "Kathy, are you coming in? I'm working on your costume. One more fitting."

In the porch room, Laurence was drawing a picture of a kitten, and Mrs H stood behind him, watching, holding a pin-cushion full of pins. "Up on the stool, Alice," she said. "I'll get this hem finished tonight."

I turned a little bit each time she jabbed my leg with a finger. Quiet filled the porch room. Mrs H had her mouth full of pins, and Laurence was concentrating on his drawing.

"Laurence, why don't you get the Lego out?" I said. "We could start another kingdom."

He spun around and, eyes wide, said, "You mean it, Kathy?"

"Sure I mean it. That kingdom was pretty neat."

Laurence leapt to his feet, dashed from the room, and thundered down the cellar steps.

I looked away from Mrs H, embarrassed by the pride glowing in her grey eyes. Laurence returned with a canister of dusty Lego, and soon the click of the plastic pieces and Laurence's contented humming filled the room.

I gazed out the window at the trees swaying in a late afternoon breeze. Tonight, I told myself, I'll go through my clothes. See what I've outgrown. See what I should pack when I leave with my mother.

Chapter Fourteen
Waiting

Saturday morning, I was up early. Friday night I thought I'd never get to sleep. Little tingles kept dashing through me, keeping me awake.

I jumped out of bed and pulled the sheets off. I'd fix everything nice in here for my mother. Tonight, I'd sleep on a cot in Laurence's room, and Jim would have the couch downstairs.

Jim. What if he didn't want me to go with them? Mrs H said it was just a visit. But I knew my mother wouldn't leave me again. After all, I wasn't a little kid any more. I could take care of myself. I wouldn't be in her way. And I'd never, never lose my temper again.

While Mrs H made chicken salad for lunch, Laurence dusted and I vacuumed, then I made blueberry muffins. Wait till my mother tasted those! After everything was ready, I went out on the front balcony to watch for her. My stomach was all a jumble and those little tingles were shooting through me again.

I sat on the wrought-iron bench and rested my arms on the railing, my chin on my hands. The day was bright green and blue, like one of Laurence's crayon drawings. Leafy trees blocked the city skyline, but I could see up the curving road towards the highway, the way my mother would come.

The morning sun was hot on my back. My eyes felt heavy. I could hardly keep them open. Thoughts drifted through my head. Would my mother be proud of me this afternoon? Would she like my singing? I tried to imagine living with her. Would we travel a lot? Where would I go to school? Maybe I could get small parts in some shows. The sun made me drowsy. My eyes closed.

I was running, running after my mother. I could almost touch her but, just as I got near, she drifted away.

Someone was rubbing my back, saying my name softly.

"Mommy?" I popped up so fast I bumped against Mrs H.

"No, Kathy. She's not here, not yet."

"Not here?"

"Not yet, Kathy. But it's getting late. It's time to have lunch and get ready."

"She's not here? Did she call? I bet she got lost. Did you give her good directions?"

Mrs H's worried grey eyes looked into mine. "I gave her very good directions. Maybe . . . maybe they got a late start."

I clenched my fists and stared at her. "She's coming. I know she is."

The three of us sat at the table, not talking much. I pushed the chicken salad around my plate and nibbled at a roll. I couldn't swallow a thing. My stomach was a cold knot. Where was my mother?

I watched Laurence spread butter on a blueberry muffin and stuff a piece in his mouth. He took a gulp of milk, leaving a white moustache. His small face narrowed in a frown and his glasses slid down his nose. "I bet her car broke down."

Mrs H didn't say anything.

The phone rang. Paralysed, I stared at it. Mrs H got

up and answered it. "Hello?" Eyebrows raised in question, she held the phone toward me. "It's Jeremiah."

I shook my head.

She nodded and turned back to the phone. "She can't talk right now, Jeremiah. Yes, I'll tell her. OK. See you tomorrow." She hung up. "He wanted to tell you to 'break a leg' and that he's looking forward to seeing the play tomorrow."

I swallowed over the tightness in my throat. "How can I do the show? I wanted to be Alice for my mother. It's for her. If . . . if she doesn't come, I can't be Alice."

Mrs H walked over to me, put her hands on my shoulders and turned me to face her. "You can be Alice, Kathy. You have to be. You can't let everybody down. They're depending on you."

"I'm depending on my mother. She said she'd come. She promised!"

Laurence pushed his glasses up and wiped his hand across his mouth. "I bet her car broke down," he repeated. "I bet she'll come."

Mrs H pulled open a drawer and rummaged for

paper and pencil. "We'll leave a note on the door. A big note with directions to the school."

Bright lights and noisy chatter filled the dressing-room as kids got into costumes and Mrs Levine applied make-up.

Jason, his big white ears standing up straight, hopped over to me, holding up a huge cardboard clock. "You're late; you're late," he sang.

Megan, in her striped Cheshire Cat costume and a wide grin painted on her face, rushed over. "Where have you been, Kathy? Mrs Levine wants to do your make-up. Hurry and get in costume."

I spotted Kim with some of the kids in flower costumes. "What's she doing here?" I whispered.

Jason stuck his face in mine. "Make-up. She did mine. Pretty good, huh?"

Megan gave him a shove. "Get lost, Jason. Tell me, Kathy. Where's your mother sitting?"

"She . . ." I started, then cleared my throat. How could I sing? My throat kept doing weird things. "She's going to be late. Mrs H and Laurence are in the second row. They're saving a seat for her."

Kim glided over. "So, your mother's not here?"

I clenched my fists and glared at her. "She's coming."

"Grow up, Kathy. She's *not* coming."

"Shut up, Kim," said Megan. "I don't know why they let you help with make-up. You shouldn't be allowed back here."

Kim lifted her long dark hair and let it slide over her shoulder. "They let me help because I'm good. Too bad I'm not Alice. They'd be sure of a *good* performance."

Anger flashed through me. I was sick of Kim and her nasty remarks. "Well, I *am* Alice. And Mr Stickles chose me because I have the *best* voice. And I'll be the *best* Alice ever." I grabbed my bag and went to change.

Out on stage, the darkened auditorium stretched before me. My stomach fluttered. I took a deep breath and began, "In my world . . ." I pictured my mother sitting out there in the dark. I sang to her.

Jason rushed out from behind the curtain, holding up his clock and singing, "I'm late. I'm late . . ." And I followed the White Rabbit into Wonderland.

Intermission. The play was half over. I couldn't believe it. I didn't want it to end. When I was on stage, excitement bubbled through me and lifted me up.

Megan, holding up her long tail, grabbed my arm. "Kathy, come on. Let's peek out. Maybe we can spot your mother."

I hesitated, suddenly afraid.

Afraid to look out.

"No," I snapped. "You can't see anything anyway. The lights blind you."

Megan looked at me quickly. Then she swept the end of her long tail against my cheek. "The show's going great. The applause was awesome! And you were great, Kathy. Really!"

Back on stage. Alice's Wonderland was getting scary. The flowers didn't want her. They called her a weed and pushed her away. The Cheshire Cat grinned, disappeared and reappeared. Alice told him she wanted to go home, but couldn't find the way.

Then it was time for my solo. I sang "I give myself very good advice, but I very seldom follow it . . . Will I ever learn to do the things I should?" As I sang, I became aware of a bond with the audience. Electric waves seemed to connect us and carry me along. I finished. A few seconds of silence, then thunderous applause.

Curtain call. We stood together on stage, arms around each other's waists, singing "Alice in Wonderland." The audience rose to its feet and the applause went on and on. Then the house lights flooded the room. People slipped on coats and jackets. In row two, I could see Mrs H and Laurence standing, applauding and applauding.

Friends and relatives were gathering in front of the stage. Kids clattered down the steps. I saw Megan, holding a big bouquet of flowers, with her mother and father. Jason jumped from the stage and swooped his little sister up, hopping around with her. She giggled and pulled on his long white ears.

I floated down the steps, still wrapped in the magic of the play. Nothing seemed real. People patted me on the back, smiled at me, congratulated me.

Mrs H and Laurence, carrying flowers, hurried over. Mrs H, tears streaming down her cheeks, crushed me to her. "You did it, Kathy. You did it. And you were wonderful!"

Pride washed over me. I had done it. I had played Alice even though . . .

We were almost at the car when Laurence pulled on my arm and said, "I bet her car broke down, Kathy. I bet she'll come. She'll see the play tomorrow."

Chapter Fifteen
Letting Go

All the way home, my body felt strange. One minute, I'd be floating, thinking of that special connection with the audience. The next, I'd be sinking – my mother hadn't come.

When Mrs H turned into the driveway, I leaned forward, searching for a strange car. Maybe my mother was there . . . waiting? No car. My heart plunged into my stomach.

The directions were still pinned to the door. I ripped them off and pushed the door open. The answering machine beeped and flashed in the kitchen. My heart lifted. Maybe Laurence was right. Maybe the car did break down. "A message, Mrs H. There's a message."

Mrs H came and stood by me. I watched her long finger push the "play" button.

The machine whirred. Then – my mother's voice.

"Listen, baby, I can't come. I thought it would be kind of fun to see you, but . . . well, this morning, Jim got a call from New York. He says it's a good opportunity for me. So we're heading south. Bye."

I stood staring at the clicking, beeping machine. Hope drained from me, leaving my body heavy, anchored to the floor. Then, screams crashed through me, freeing me. "I hate her! I hate her!"

I burst out the door, flew down the steps, leaped over the garden plot, and up the stone stairs.

I ran past the apple trees, up, up, up the hill.

At the edge of the woods, I fell to the ground, howling.

Tearing great clumps of grass up by the roots, I wailed, "I hate her! I hate her!"

Mrs H, breathing hard, knelt beside me. She held me to her in a vice-like hug, forcing my hands to still, forcing my face into the soft skin of her warm, damp, neck. I struggled but I couldn't move. Finally, I leaned into her and sank against her cushiony chest.

"Hating hurts," she murmured.

The loss and fear I'd felt as a six-year-old washed over me. In a hoarse whisper, I sobbed, "I hate my mother, I hate her . . . but . . . but I love my mother . . .

I can't hate her. But she left me. Why? Why? What's wrong with me?"

"There's nothing wrong with you, not one little thing," said Mrs H, rocking me back and forth like a baby. "And you don't hate your mother, not really. You hate what she did to you. You hate that she left you. Now, you go ahead and cry. It will make you feel better."

Tears welled out of my eyes and streamed down my face. Mrs H cradled me against her. Her blouse, soaked with my tears, was wet against my cheek. It smelled of cinnamon. Mrs H, her chin nestled against my head, murmured in her deep, soothing voice.

"It hurts. It hurts a lot to have your mother leave you. But it doesn't mean you're unlovable. It means your mother isn't loving. She can't love the way you do or the way I love you. And that's not your fault."

"Then she didn't love me . . . she never loved me at all?" As I said the words, I knew it was true. All the dreams I'd had about her coming back were just fantasies, like Laurence's Lego kingdom, like his dream about Mrs H and Mr Tyler, like Alice's Wonderland. Understanding swept through me like pain, and with it a surge of powerful anger. "I'm glad she's not coming. I don't want to see her, not ever."

Hot tears flowed from my eyes and I cried as though my mother were dead.

After a time, I sat back and blew my nose with some tissues Mrs H had in her pocket. "Maisie's not a good mother either," I said. "She wouldn't nurse Foster."

"Maybe she didn't have enough milk for eight kittens."

"So Marmalade took care of him, like you take care of Laurence and me."

Mrs H squeezed my shoulders. "She adopted him, like I want to adopt you, just like I did Laurence."

I shifted my position and looked up into her face. "You *really* do?"

"I *really* do," she said, brushing strands of hair off my forehead. "But it's up to you, and we have plenty of time to talk about it. You have to let go of your past . . . your mother first, then we can move on to the future."

"That's what Mrs Cruz always says . . . but . . ."

"But?"

"I hate to think of my mother as a terrible person."

"Not a terrible person, Kathy. She was very young when she had you, and maybe she just can't grow up. I bet you have some good memories from when you lived with her."

I searched my mind; it was such a long time ago.

Then I remembered. "Sometimes she would brush my hair and sing a song. I liked that."

"That sounds like a good memory to store in your memory box."

Mrs H heaved herself to her feet and brushed grass and twigs from her slacks. "Goodness, my legs are stiff," she said. "Let's sit over here for a few minutes."

We sat without talking on a fallen log. I picked up a twig and twirled it, watching the dancing shadows the westward sun made through the apple trees. Then a frightening thought came. "What if I'm like her? What if I have a baby some day and leave it?"

"Do you think you'd do that?"

I thought of how Marmalade had licked and cleaned her newborn kittens, how she protected them. "No," I said, shaking my head. "I'd be like you and Marmalade. I'd take real good care of my baby."

"I know you would," said Mrs H, lifting my chin and looking into my eyes. I looked back into her clear grey eyes and a warm feeling spread through me. I felt like Alice, coming out of Wonderland, where everything was confusing and frightening.

"You know," I said, as we walked back to the house, "when Laurence threw Bozo in the fire, it was like part of my mother died. Now it seems like she really has died."

"Oh, Kathy, I guess in a way she has for you and, in a way, that's not bad. If you can remember the good things about her, maybe the bad things won't hurt so much."

Just ahead of us, my apple tree glowed in the setting sun. Soon its buds would blossom into beautiful white flowers. And I would be here to see them. I reached out and slipped my hand into Mrs H's.

Published by Poolbeg

The Caribbean Jewels Mystery

by

Joyce A. Stengel

When fourteen-year-old Cassie Hartt joins her father and new stepmother and stepsister for a holiday on board *The Seabird,* a luxury Caribbean cruise liner bound for Martinique, she finds it difficult to sort out complicated feelings for her father and his new family.

Bored, Cassie attends a lecture in which she is shown the "Jewelled Jesu" – an ancient statue featuring a tiny image of Christ surrounded by gems – and is fascinated by the legend of an Indian maiden who, centuries earlier, vanished into a cave high in the mountains of Martinique where the Jewelled Jesu was found.

Cassie also discovers a romantic interest in Charles Nobre Reyes, a handsome but mysterious young man she meets on board the ship. Circumstances fling the teenagers together when the Jewelled Jesu goes missing and an exciting race against time ensues to recover the stolen statue and bring it to its rightful resting place.

An exciting mystery set against a backdrop of exotic locations.

ISBN: 1-85371-661-8

Published by Poolbeg

Anna's Six Wishes

by

MARGRIT CRUICKSHANK

Illustrated by Marie Louise Fitzpatrick

Anna didn't believe in Fairy Godmothers. Not many people do, nowadays. And then this spider walked out from behind her book . . .

Anna only got six wishes "for the rest of her life". And it's not easy to make the perfect wish. What would you wish for?

A six chapter "Easy Reader" book featuring large type, simple language and charming illustrations by Marie Louise Fitzpatrick. The perfect book for readers aged 6 – 9.

ISBN: 1-85371-510-7

Published by Poolbeg

LIZA'S LAMB

BY

MARGRIT CRUICKSHANK

ILLUSTRATED BY LAURA CRONIN

Shane's leg suddenly becomes sore, for no reason he can think of, and the doctor tells him he has to go to hospital, miles and miles away, up in Dublin! So, when there is an emergency back home on the farm and his mother has to leave him on his own, he doesn't want to talk to anyone – especially not the red-haired girl who shares his cubicle and talks non-stop!

Gradually Shane settles into the routine of hospital and he and Liza become friends. One day, he even promises her one of his Daddy's lambs for her very own pet. But how can you give a lamb to someone who lives in a small city house?

A reassuring book for 6 – 11 year-olds describing a stay in hospital.

ISBN: 1-85371-518-2